This Storybook Belongs to:

Princess _____

Cinderella

A Royal Heart

Enchanted Moments

ADVANCE PUBLISHERS

The girls at Madame Bertrand's school settled into a circle around their teacher, ready to begin another day's lessons.

"I have a very special surprise for you this morning," their teacher told them.

"What is it?" the girls clamored excitedly.

As if in answer, the clip-clopping of hooves approached on the cobblestone road outside.

"I wonder who that could be?" said Madame Bertrand with a mysterious smile.

Unable to contain their curiousity, the girls all raced to the window.

"It's the royal carriage!" they cried.

Moments later, Madame Bertrand greeted their visitor with a curtsy. "Good day to you, Princess Cinderella," she said. "We appreciate you coming by to see us today.

"Good day to you, Madame," Cinderella replied. "I am delighted to be here. I have been looking forward to visiting with the girls all week."

Cinderella gave the teacher some baskets filled with freshly baked treats, then turned to the class of girls who stood speechless nearby.

"Girls," Madame Bertrand prompted, "aren't you going to welcome our guest?"

One of the students rushed forward immediately. "Hello, Princess Cinderella," she said breathlessly. "My name is Katie and I think you're beautiful!"

"Why, thank you," said Cinderella. "I am very pleased to meet all of you. Your teacher has graciously allowed me to come and read a story to you today."

But as Cinderella reached for a book off the shelf, Katie protested. "Princess Cinderella, can you please tell us about what it's like to be a princess? That's more interesting than any story in a book!"

"What would you like to know?" Cinderella asked.
The girls' questions came out in a tumble:

"How many fancy gowns do you have?"

"When do you wear your tiara?"

"Do your pets have thrones too?"

Cinderella laughed as she pictured her horse sitting on a giant gilded chair!

After the Princess had told the girls a little bit about her life at the castle, they were ready to settle down for their schoolwork. Cinderella helped Mrs. Bertrand with the lessons, then they all shared the cakes and cookies the Princess had brought.

"Thank you for a lovely time," Cinderella said when it was time to leave. She always loved meeting and spending time with the people who lived in her kingdom, and today was no exception.

That afternoon, Katie couldn't stop thinking about their surprise visitor
and what it would be like to be a real, live princess. She imagined days filled
with dress fittings and tea parties, and evenings attending one fancy ball
after another.

Hoping to catch another glimpse of Cinderella, Katie took a walk to the castle.

"How I wish that I could go inside," she thought as she stood gazing up at the
gates. "It must be beautiful."

Then, to Katie's surprise, the gates swung open!

"You may enter," called the guard.

Suddenly, a group of seamstresses swept past her. Without even thinking, Katie slipped among the group and walked in with them!

Once inside the enormous castle, Katie watched as Cinderella approached one of the seamstresses. The little girl ducked behind a curtain and listened as the two women discussed the details of some new ball gowns that were being made for the Princess.

"I have to see them!" Katie decided. "They must be exquisite!"

When Cinderella and the seamstress parted, Katie came out from her hiding place. The little girl headed down the hallway after the seamstress and soon heard the clacking of knitting needles and the snipping of scissors.

Unable to resist, Katie poked her head in the doorway—much to the surprise of the ladies working there.

"Hello," Katie ventured. "I'm a friend of Cinderella's—and . . . um . . . she sent me here to check on her ball gowns."

"Really?" asked one of the ladies kindly.

"No," admitted Katie, "but may I see them anyway?"

"I don't see why not," said the seamstress, looking at Katie's eager face.

The woman opened a wardrobe to reveal gowns of jewel-colored silk, velvet, and taffeta.

"They're not finished," explained the seamstress. "But when they are, these gowns will be fit for a princess."

"But they're fit for a princess now," Katie gasped. "I wish I had a dress as pretty as one of these."

"We have plenty of extra fabric," said the seamstress. "Would you like us to make you one?"

Following Katie's direction, the ladies cut and sewed. When Cinderella appeared a few hours later, she was surprised to see her new friend—and even more surprised by Katie's unusual gown!

A little while later, Cinderella and Katie sat down for tea.

"What brings you to the castle?" Cinderella asked.

"I had to see what being a princess is like for myself," replied Katie. "It must be wonderful to wear sparkling jewels and be surrounded by servants and to go to fancy balls all the time."

Cinderella smiled. "You know, Katie," she said gently, "All those things *are* wonderful, but princesses do more than dress up and go to parties. They take care of the people in their kingdom by getting to know them and making sure they have what they need."

Katie furrowed her brow as she thought for a moment. "That sounds like hard work."

Cinderella smiled. "Actually, sometimes it is, but it's the kind of hard work that makes you feel good inside."

"Then I still want to be a princess when I grow up," Katie declared firmly.

"Then you had better practice," replied Cinderella. "Follow me."

Cinderella took Katie to a playroom that contained a wardrobe filled with dress-up clothes and jewelry.

"Let's play princess," suggested Cinderella. "You be the princess and I will be one of the people in your kingdom."

Then—to Katie's disbelief—Cinderella turned to her and curtsied!

When there game was over, Cinderella summoned the royal carriage to take Katie back to Madame Bertrand's. All the way there, Katie and Cinderella looked out the window of the carriage and waved to the people they saw. Katie loved how everyone smiled and waved in return.

"The people in our kingdom seem very happy," thought Katie. "If I ever get to be a princess, I'm going to take care of my subjects just the way Cinderella takes care of hers."

Before Cinderella said goodbye, she had one last treat in store for the girls.

"You are all invited to a party in your honor at noon tomorrow," she said. "I do hope you'll come!"

When the girls and Madame Bertrand arrived at the castle at the appointed hour, there was another surprise waiting for them. Each guest had a beautiful custom-made dress waiting for her—and a butler to fetch them whatever they needed!

The afternoon was filled with dancing and delicious food and games and laughter.

When the festivities were over, Cinderella had a special announcement to make to Katie and the other girls.

"I am in need of some honorary princesses to help me with my work in the kingdom—and I think I know some young ladies who might just be perfect for the job," she told them.

From then on, the girls often went with Cinderella as she traveled throughout the land. They cheered up the sick, delivered food to the needy, and offered friendship to all.

They were also frequent guests at the castle, where they might play with the servants' children, enjoy the dress-up clothes in the playroom, or join Cinderella for tea. Katie loved being an honorary princess—but she loved being Cinderella's friend even more!